Cowboy Cal

by Jim Kraft
illustrated by Eldon Doty

Troll

For Jean, Jeff, and Matt
—J.K.

Unless your head's been stuck down a prairie-dog hole, you've probably heard about Cowboy Cal, the world's greatest kid-cowboy. And you've probably heard about Buster, Cal's fabulous horse. But if you *haven't* heard, then it's time you did.

One day, Cowboy Cal and Buster were out riding the range. They trotted for miles under the broad blue sky, while Cal sang his favorite cowboy song over and over.

Buster rolled his eyes, which was his way of saying, *If I hear that song one more time, I'm gonna go loco!*

Outside a little prairie town, Cal saw children playing. "Baseball! Yee-ha!" whooped Cal. "That's more fun than wrestling a rattlesnake. I think I'll join in."

"Neigh," added Buster, which is a horse's way of saying, *You hit the baseball, I'll hit the lemonade stand.*

Naturally, Cal was as great a ballplayer as he was a cowboy. He ran the bases faster than a jackrabbit (assuming jackrabbits know how to run the bases, which has never been proven).

Cal was so good with his lariat, he didn't need a glove. He could rope the highest fly right out of the sky.

whack!

The score was tied in the bottom of the ninth, and Cal was coming up to bat. Suddenly, swirling and curling over the western mountaintops came the biggest, angriest thundercloud anyone had ever seen.

"Now we'll never finish our game!" some of the children wailed. Others trembled at the lightning and thunder.

Cowboy Cal turned to his horse. "Buster, we've got to do something," he said. Buster nodded, which meant, *Right! I'll race you to the storm cellar.*

Cal vaulted into the saddle and grabbed the reins. "Head straight for that thundercloud, Buster!"

Buster stared at Cal, as if to say, *Cal, old pal, you are the best and bravest kid-cowboy in the world. But have you completely lost your marbles?*

Despite Buster's doubts, horse and rider were soon streaking across the stormy plain.

"Faster, Buster! Faster!" urged Cal. "Race for the top of the tallest mountain!"

Up the side of the mountain they roared. By the time they reached the peak, Cal and Buster were no more than a blur. And then suddenly . . .

. . . they were airborne! Buster was so surprised, he was speechless. They rose like a rainbow, soaring toward the stormcloud, which crackled furiously and fired a blast of hail.

Cal ignored the iceballs. Swinging his lariat, he twirled a loop around his head. "Easy as roping catfish," he said, letting the loop fly.

The rope snagged the whipping tail of the stormcloud. With a yank, Cal pulled the loop tight.

"Now for a nice soft landing," he said. Buster twitched his ears, which meant, *Nope, we're gonna plummet to Earth like a meteor and make a major splat!*

But the stormcloud acted like a hot-air balloon. Cal and Buster floated gently to the ground.

"I know just the place for this monster," Cal declared. "Buster, head for the Great Gritty Desert."

It hadn't rained in the Great Gritty Desert for one hundred years. All the cacti were dying of thirst, and the lizards were eating dust soup.

Cal and Buster dragged the storm to the middle of the desert. "Great Gritty," said Cal, "you can say 'good-bye' to the dry." He jerked hard on the rope. The tail of the stormcloud tore away, and out poured a river of rainwater.

The Great Gritty Desert turned green. The cacti drank till their barrels were full. Gila monsters paddled in the pools. Buster himself took a long sip of water (though he would have preferred lemonade).

With the storm subdued and the desert blooming, Cal and Buster returned to the prairie town.

"Hooray for the heroes!" the children cried.

Cowboy Cal tipped his hat, while Buster signed autographs.

The baseball game resumed, but unfortunately Cowboy Cal struck out. That happens sometimes, even to the best.

That night, Cal and Buster returned to the Double-C Ranch.

"Great job today," said Cal, tucking Buster into bed. "You are definitely the best horse in the world."

Buster snorted, which meant, *Then I think I deserve breakfast in bed tomorrow. And by the way, you're pretty terrific yourself.*

Cowboy Cal turned out the light and slid under the covers. He lay in the darkness, softly humming his favorite cowboy song, while Buster snored contentedly. Which is a horse's way of saying . . . THE END.